# BEARYMORE

# BEARYMORE

Story and pictures by

## DON FREEMAN

PUFFIN BOOKS

# To Nicholas

Penguin Books Ltd, Harmondsworth, Middlesex, England
Penguin Books, 625 Madison Avenue, New York, New York 10022, U.S.A.
Penguin Books Australia Ltd, Ringwood, Victoria, Australia
Penguin Books Canada Limited, 2801 John Street, Markham, Ontario, Canada L3R 1B4
Penguin Books (N.Z.) Ltd, 182–190 Wairau Road, Auckland 10, New Zealand

First published by The Viking Press 1976
Published in Puffin Books 1979

Library of Congress Cataloging in Publication Data
Freeman, Don.    Bearymore.
Summary: A circus bear has trouble hibernating
and dreaming up a new act at the same time.
[1. Bears—Fiction. 2. Circus stories] I. Title.
PZ7.F8747Be 1979      [E]      78-18281
ISBN 0 14 050.279 3

Printed in the United States of America by
Rae Publishing Co., Inc., Cedar Grove, New Jersey
Set in Cheltenham Old Style

One November night under the big top an excited crowd cheered the performers louder than usual.

It was the last show of the season. Soon everyone connected with the circus would be going south to bask in the sun, everyone except Bearymore, the performing bear. He planned to go into hibernation for the winter, as he did every year.

Bearymore felt sad when he made his final bow.
He loved the circus so much he wished it could continue
all year round.

Later that night the ringmaster took Bearymore aside for a serious chat. "I'm sorry to tell you this, Beary," he said, "but if you want to stay with our circus next season you will have to work up a new act. Just riding around the ring on that unicycle is getting to be old hat."

Bearymore understood, but he was worried. How could he possibly create a new act and hibernate at the same time?

For the moment, however, Bearymore was unable to keep
his mind on such a difficult problem. His friends had gathered
in front of his private wagon to say good-bye.

Fantella, the elephant, gave him a fancy pillow as a hibernating present.

Bearymore was touched. "Thank you very much," he said wistfully. "I hope to see you all in the spring."

Then he hung his unicycle on the telephone pole, took his nightshirt off the laundry line, and went into his wagon.

A few minutes later he tacked a sign on the door outside.

While the clowns removed their make-up, the roustabouts quickly folded the canvas tent and loaded it onto a freight car.

A special train was waiting to transport the entire circus to its winter quarters in Florida.

"I hate to hibernate," grumbled Bearymore as he crawled into bed, "but this is what we bears have to do, so the sooner I go to sleep the sooner spring will come."

It wasn't very long before he began to toss and turn. "Oh,
I almost forgot," he said, suddenly sitting up. "I've got to
think of an idea for my new act. Maybe some music will help
inspire me."

He hopped out of bed, wound up his old-fashioned phonograph, and put on a record of lively circus music.

Bearymore danced around the floor, flapping his arms and clapping his paws.

He then tried balancing a ball on the end of his nose as he climbed up and down a ladder.

Unfortunately, everything he thought of doing had been done before, only better, by his friends the performing seals.

When the phonograph finally wound down, Bearymore fell
into bed, exhausted and discouraged.

Still, he wasn't able to sleep a wink because of a tickle in
his throat. "A bear can't sleep if he's thirsty," he growled.

He got up and trotted outdoors to the water pump to get a drink.

There wasn't a trace of the circus anywhere, only a lonely vacant lot.

Bearymore went back inside and again crawled under the covers.

All at once he remembered something else. "How will I know when it's time for me to get up?" he said, scratching his fuzzy head. "Oh, I know! I'll wind up my clock."

He set the alarm for April.

But Bearymore still had trouble going to sleep.
"Oh, well," he grunted, "I have all winter long to think
of something for my new act..." But before he finished this
sentence, his eyes closed. He had finally fallen asleep.

Outside soft snowflakes gradually covered the wagon.
Days and weeks and months passed slowly by.

While he slept Bearymore dreamed that his circus friends were having fun sunning themselves around a ring-shaped pool.

Fantella was there floating on a huge rubber pillow and happily fanning herself. "I wonder what our friend Beary is doing?" she was saying to Speedy Zebra.

"Oh, he's probably working on his new act," replied Speedy, splashing about.

Just then a large gold telephone began to ring. It rang louder
and louder. "Why doesn't Fantella answer the phone?"
wondered Bearymore in his sleep.

Of course there was a very good reason....

It wasn't a telephone ringing, it was his own alarm clock telling him to wake up.

Today was the first of April.

Bearymore awoke with a start. "I must have dozed off for a minute," he said, turning off the alarm. "Oh, no! It can't be April already. The circus will be back soon, and I haven't yet thought of an idea for my new act."

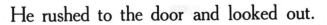

He rushed to the door and looked out.

A morning spring rain was drizzling. "Just look at that. I forgot to bring in my unicycle!" he exclaimed. "It will get all rusty if I leave it out there any longer."

The ground was slippery and muddy. Bearymore wasn't about to get soaking wet, so he opened his umbrella and climbed the ladder up to the roof of his wagon.

Without hesitating a second, he walked across on the laundry line, balancing himself perfectly, step by step.

When he reached the telephone pole he carefully leaned
down and picked up his unicycle. "I certainly can't ride through
all that mud," he muttered to himself. He decided to pedal
all the way back on the laundry line.

Bearymore had started to do this with the greatest of ease
when suddenly, midway across,

he glanced down and saw his reflection in the water. "I've got it!" he roared. "I see the idea for my new act!"

In his excitement Bearymore lost his balance and over he fell...

KERSPLASH! right smack into the middle of the puddle.

Bearymore didn't mind where he had landed. His problem was solved! And as he sat grinning, he heard the sound of a train whistle far in the distance.

His friends were returning from their Florida vacation!

Soon the rain let up and the sun came out in all its glory.
This meant the circus could open that night as planned.

While the roustabouts were busily putting up the tent,
Fantella gave Bearymore a much-needed shower bath.

"Well, Beary, have you worked up a new act?" asked the ringmaster during supper. "We're counting on you, don't forget."

Bearymore beamed as only a bear hiding a secret can beam. "Wait and see," he said. "Just give me a highwire and a net."

Promptly at eight that evening the first show of the season got under way.

When Bearymore heard the noisy crowd and the sound of band music, his ears perked up. And when he smelled the popcorn and cotton candy he could hardly wait to perform.

As he began to climb the rope ladder higher and higher, the ringmaster announced, "LADIES AND GENTLE-MEN! We now proudly present the one and only Amazing Bearymore, in a new act never before seen by anyone in the world!"

The audience grew very quiet. All the circus performers were spellbound as the drummer played a long, loud drum roll....

The ringmaster's mouth dropped open when he saw the daring young bear riding his unicycle on the highwire all the way from pole to pole, without once needing the net!

The applause was thunderous.

Yes, Bearymore's new act was a spectacular success. Overnight he had become a great star.

And never again did he have any trouble hibernating.